For my dear friend
Jo Coleman
with love

First published in hardback
by HarperCollins Publishers USA in 2013

This edition first published in paperback in the UK
by HarperCollins Children's Books in 2014

1 3 5 7 9 10 8 6 4 2

ISBN: 978-0-00-748355-6

HarperCollins Children's Books is a division of HarperCollins Publishers Ltd.

Copyright © Emma Dodd 2013

Visit our website at www.harpercollins.co.uk

Printed and bound in China

Emma DODD

Foxy in love

HarperCollins *Children's Books*

It was almost Valentine's Day. Emily was making a special card, but she was having trouble deciding what to draw.

Just then, Foxy appeared at the window.

"What are you doing?" he asked Emily.

"Hello, Foxy. I'm trying to think of all the things I love so I can draw them in my card," said Emily. "But I love everything! I don't know where to start."

Foxy was sure he could help.
"Think hard, Emily," he said.
"What do you love best of all?"

"Oh yes! I know!" said Emily.

"Of course you do,"
Foxy said, smiling shyly.

"I love **balloons!**" Emily said.

"Balloons!" said Foxy with a sigh. He was very disappointed, but he waved his magical tail back and forth and back and forth anyway.

"Ta-da!
Balloons!"

Emily laughed. "Those are **racoons, not balloons!**"

Foxy tried again, and this time he filled
the room with colourful balloons.

"Oh, thank you, Foxy!" exclaimed Emily.

"You're welcome," Foxy said. "Now, can
you think of something else you love?"

Emily thought for a moment.
"I love pots of **hot chocolate-**
with **marshmallows!**"

Foxy wasn't sure he heard her correctly. But he swished his tail, and suddenly there was a . . .

. . . bathtub full of **hot chocolate** and **marshmallows!**

"That's lots of hot chocolate!" she said. "I just wanted a pot!
Never mind, Foxy. I thought of something else."

"You did?" asked Foxy hopefully.

"I love **flowers**!" Emily said.
"Flowers?" Foxy sighed again and
waved his tail. "Coming right up!"

Emily giggled. "Not this kind of **flour,** Foxy!
The kind that grows in the ground!"

Even Foxy laughed. "Whoops!"
A swish of his tail, and the floor was
a garden of beautiful flowers.

"Ooh . . . I love rainbows," said Emily.
"Anything else?" asked Foxy, still hopeful.

"And **umbrellas**,"
added Emily.

"I know I will need a lot of **hearts!**" Emily said.

"No, not **larks!**
Not **tarts!**"

"That's better!"

Foxy loved all the hearts, but
something was still missing.
"Emily, I think you forgot
something important," said Foxy.

"But Foxy, I don't have room to draw anything else on this Valentine's Day card."

"Valentine's Day is not about *what* you love," Foxy explained. "It's about *who* you love."